By Jenny Phillips

Illustrated by Kessler Garrity

Cover Design by Phillip Colhouer

goodandbeautiful.com

# CHAPTERS

## Challenge Words

friend

new

storm

# CHAPTER 1

## Mark's New Home

This was Mark's home. It had tall trees by it.

Mark is going to a new home with his mother and father.

Look! There is Mark's new home—Mars, the Red Planet.

Mark's new home is a dome. Do you like it?

It has no trees by it, but it has a ton of red sand.

Mark has so much fun looking at his new small home.

He goes up the
steps. He slides
down the pole.

Mark sleeps here.
His bed is soft and warm.
He stares at the
stars in the black,
black sky.

He also sees. . . TWO moons!

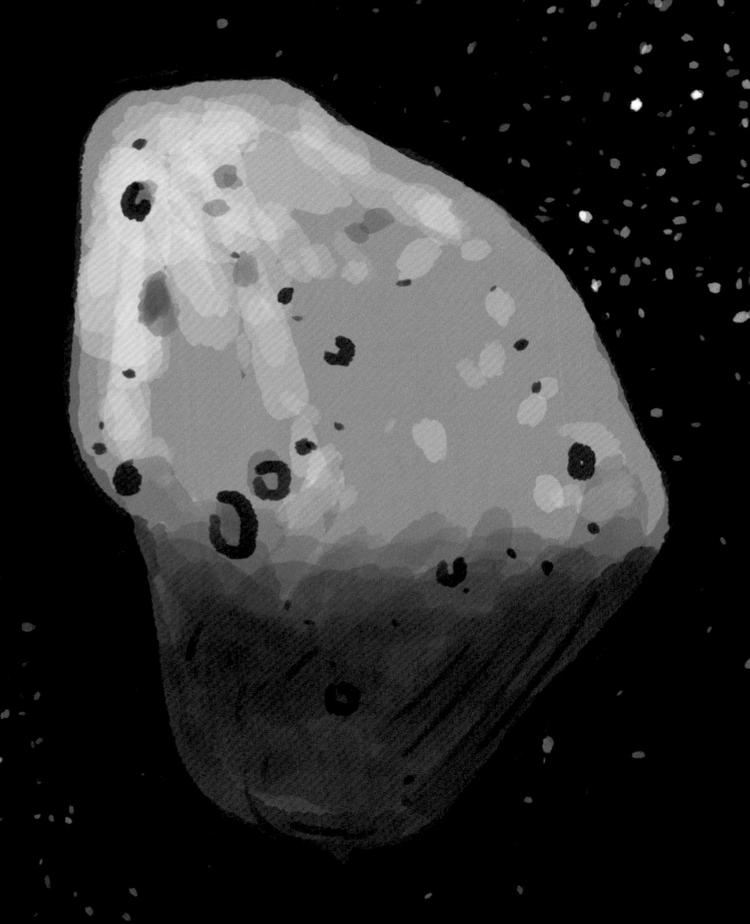

Look at how they are shaped! They are small moons.

Mark wakes up. His dad greets him with a smile.

“Let’s go on a drive!” says Dad. Mark jumps up to go.

# CHAPTER 2

## Mark's Drive

Mark's dad has a job. He makes maps of Mars.

Mark and his dad speed on the flat land.

"Weee!" says Mark. "This is the best!"

Mark sees hills and cliffs. He sees small and big rocks.

The sky looks red, and the land looks red and tan.

Mark and his dad see a volcano that is SO tall!

It is taller than any volcano they have ever seen.

Mark’s dad is making maps of sand dunes.

They go on for miles, and miles, and miles.

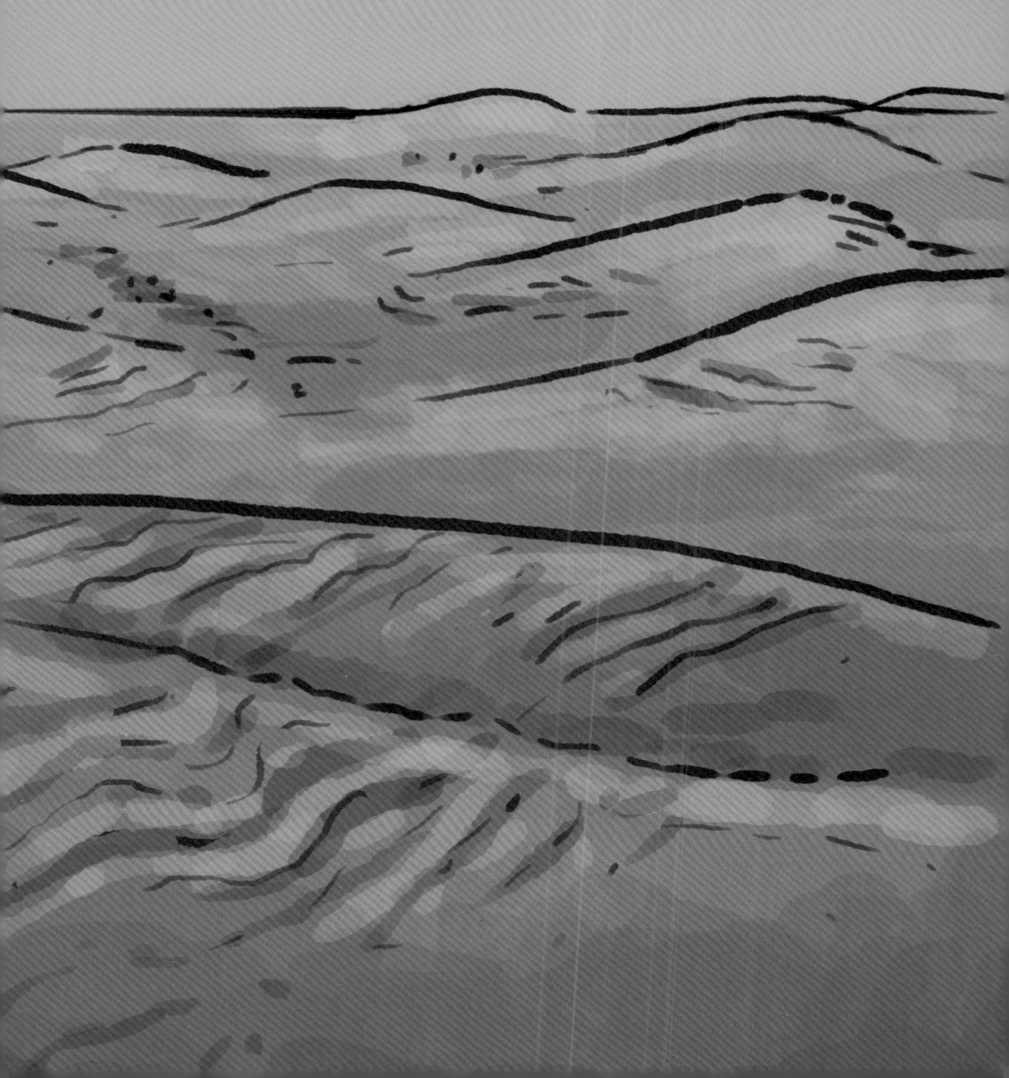

Mark has a mask.
All people on Mars
have masks.

In their homes, they take the masks off.

Mark jumps. Wow! He jumps three feet into the sky.

It is so fun to jump on Mars!

# CHAPTER 3

## A Rock Hits Mars

One day Mark feels his home rocking just a little.

A big rock has hit Mars. It is not close to Mark's

home, but it still rocked the home.

The next day, Mark and his family go to see the hole that the rock made.

It is such a deep hole!

A lot of rocks hit Mars, but often they are small. As they drive home, Mark looks at small holes all over the land.

Mark is glad
that big rocks
do not hit Mars
often.

He feels safe and
snug in his bed.

# CHAPTER 4

## The Big Storm

Mars has storms—BIG dust storms. The wind is strong and the sky is filled with dust.

Some dust storms are so big that all of the planet is in the storm. This is an epic storm!

One day a dust storm starts, and Mark and his family have to stay in their home.

Strong winds make the storm bigger and bigger.

Three weeks go by, and
the storm is still there.

This is a hard part of living on Mars.

# CHAPTER 5

## Life on Mars

Five weeks pass, and the storm fades.

Mark can go out of his home. He is so glad the storm is done.

It can be hard to live on Mars, but Mark likes it.

He loves to see the big ships come and go.

He loves to plant seeds
and see the new plants

Taking care of chickens is

He loves to read books.

He has a shelf with seven books, and he trades books with his friend Pam.

Driving with his dad and helping him make maps is so much fun. They are pals.

And the sunsets on Mars. . . well, they are just stunning! In the day, the dust-filled sky is red. As the sun sets, the sky turns blue

Mark looks at the sunset and smiles. “I like my home on Mars,” he says.